R0200882397

01/2020

THE BOXCAR CHILDREN®

MIKE'S MYSTERY

Library of Congress Cataloging-in-Publication data is on file with the publisher.

Printed in the United States of America
10 9 8 7 6 5 4 3 2 1 LB 24 23 22 21 20 19

Cover and interior art by Shane Clester

Visit the Boxcar Children online at www.boxcarchildren.com.
For more information about Albert Whitman & Company,
visit our website at www.albertwhitman.com.

100 Years of Albert Whitman & Company
Celebrate with us in 2019!

THE BOXCAR CHILDREN®

MIKE'S MYSTERY

Based on the book by
Gertrude Chandler Warner

Albert Whitman & Company
Chicago, Illinois

"It all changed!" said Violet.
The Aldens were visiting
Aunt Jane.
Her house was once
on a big ranch.
Now it was by a big town.
"The mine has brought so
many people to Yellow Sands,"
said Jessie.
"Let's explore!" said Benny.

Henry, Jessie, Violet, and Benny
loved to explore.
The children had once lived
in a boxcar.
At the time, they did not
have a home.
But they did have many
adventures.

Then Grandfather found them.
Now they had a real home.
They still had many adventures!

It did not take long to find their first surprise.

Benny saw someone he knew!

"This is my old friend, Mike Wood," Benny said.

"Hey, I'm not old," Mike said. "We are the same age!"

Henry and Jessie knew Mike.
They also knew how much
Mike and Benny liked to argue.

Mike's brother worked
at the mine.
That was why Mike's family
had moved to Yellow Sands.
"I know everyone around here,"
said Mike.
"See? That's me in the paper."
"Oh yeah?" said Benny.
"Who is that in the funny hat?"
Mike had never seen
that man before.
"That man is a stranger,"
said Mike.
"He does not count."
"Does too!" said Benny.

The two argued all the way
to Mike's house.

Mike's mother knew just
what to do.
She set four pies on the table.
Mike and Benny could not
argue with full mouths.

"Mrs. Wood, you should be
a baker," Violet said.
"I love to make pies for my
neighbors," said Mrs. Wood.
"But the only jobs here are
with the mine.
I do laundry for the workers."

As soon as the children were done eating, Mike and Benny started up again.

"I bet Watch is faster than Spotty," said Benny.

"No way!" said Mike.

"Spotty would win a race."

Jessie stopped them.

They'd had enough excitement for one day, she said.

But there would be much more excitement that night…

The Aldens heard the news
in the morning.
There had been a fire!
Firefighters put out the flames.
But the damage was done.
Three buildings had burned.
Two were buildings for
the mine.
One was Mike's pink house!

Spotty ran up.

Mike and his mother were with him.

They were all safe.

But they had lost everything.

"I cannot work," said Mrs. Wood.

"And we do not have any place to live."

The Aldens knew what it was like not to have a home.

Violet wanted to help.

But she did not yet know how.

"We think the fire was started by a person," said Mr. Carter. He was the investigator. "Did you see anything?" "No, but Spotty did!" said Mike. Spotty had barked in the night. He woke them all up to escape the fire!

"Do you know who might have started the fire?" asked Henry. Mr. Carter shook his head. "That is a mystery."

Everyone was talking about
the fire.

"I heard the boy in that
pink house started it,"
a woman at the diner said.

She was talking about Mike!

Benny marched over.

"My friend did not start
any fire!"

The woman apologized.

She said she had heard the
story from a man in a blue hat.

Could that be who really
started the fire?

The children looked
all over town.
Then they looked at the mine.
Not one person was wearing
a blue hat.
"It looks like a dead end,"
said Mr. Carter.

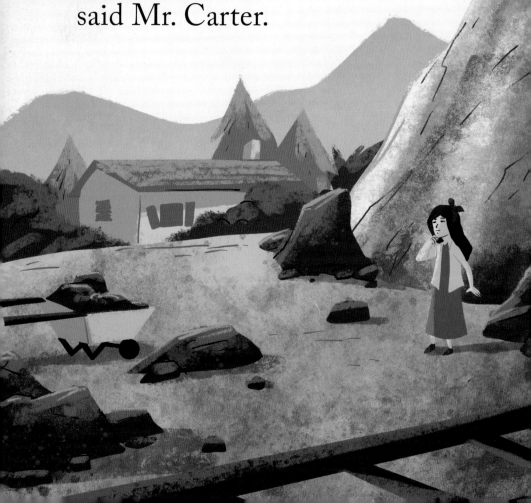

But their trip did give Violet
an idea.

It might not solve the mystery.

But it would help in another way.

That night, Violet told Henry,
Jessie, and Benny her plan.
They would need a little help.
So the children called
Grandfather.
"What a wonderful idea!"
he said.
Then the Aldens went to
the neighbors.
They were glad to help too.

The next day, the children had
a surprise for Mrs. Wood.
"We want to buy you a big
oven," Violet said.
"And dishes too."
"For your bakery!" said Benny.
"Bakery?" said Mrs. Wood.
"I do not even have a house."

But the children had a plan for that as well.

"You can stay here," said Violet.
"You can sell your pies to
the mine workers."
The building was not much.
But Mrs. Wood's neighbors
helped with that.
"It's the least we can do...
For all the times you have
baked for us."

The children had not solved the mystery.
But things were getting back to normal.
That meant Benny and Mike started to argue again.

Finally, they had their race.
Spotty and Watch lined up
at one end of the field.
Henry stood at the other.
"Go!" he called.

Watch was ahead.
Then Spotty was ahead.
Then they both stopped
and started to dig.

They found a blue hat and
a box of matches!
"The man in the hat must
know we're looking for him,"
Henry said.
"He must be the one who
started the fire!"
But what did the man look like?

Mike had an idea.
He had seen the funny looking
hat before...
in the newspaper!

"That is the man in the
blue hat!" said Mike.
"He started the fire!"
Mr. Carter nodded.
"I know this man.
He tried to buy the land
where Yellow Sands is.
He must have been upset
he did not get it!"

The next night, there was
a big party.
Mike's family had a new home.
Yellow Sands had a new bakery.

Mrs. Wood thanked the Aldens for their help.

"I just wish we had found the man in the blue hat," said Mike.

All of a sudden, Spotty barked.

He ran off.

When the children caught up, Spotty had chased someone down.

It was the man from the photo!

"Spotty must have seen him on the night of the fire," said Mike. "That is why he ran after him."

Mr. Carter grabbed the man.
"Well done," he told the children.
"You Aldens sure know how
to solve mysteries."

The children looked at
one another.

"We did not do much this time,"
said Jessie.

"It was Mike and Spotty
who figured it out."

This time, Benny did not argue.

They all agreed...

It was Mike's mystery.

Keep reading with the Boxcar Children!

Henry, Jessie, Violet, and Benny used to live in a Boxcar. Now they have adventures everywhere they go! Adapted from the beloved chapter book series, these early readers allow kids to begin reading with the stories that started it all.

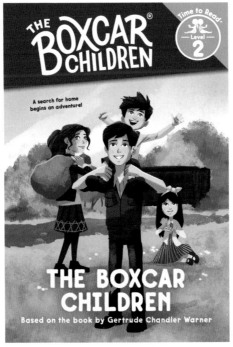

HC 978-0-8075-0839-8 · US $12.99
PB 978-0-8075-0835-0 · US $3.99

HC 978-0-8075-7675-5 · US $12.99
PB 978-0-8075-7679-3 · US $3.99

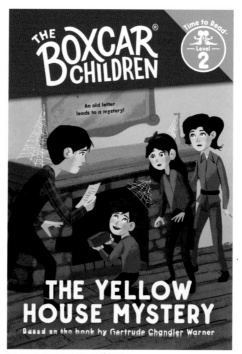

HC 978-0-8075-9367-7 · US $12.99
PB 978-0-8075-9370-7 · US $3.99

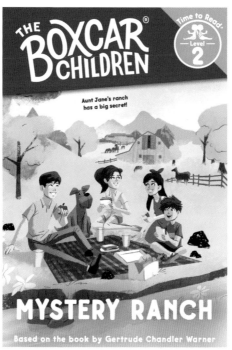

Aunt Jane's ranch
has a big secret!

MYSTERY RANCH

Based on the book by Gertrude Chandler Warner

HC 978-0-8075-5402-9 · US $12.99
PB 978-0-8075-5435-7 · US $3.99

GERTRUDE CHANDLER WARNER discovered when she was teaching that many readers who like an exciting story could find no books that were both easy and fun to read. She decided to try to meet this need, and her first book, *The Boxcar Children*, quickly proved she had succeeded.

Miss Warner drew on her own experiences to write the mystery. As a child she spent hours watching trains go by on the tracks opposite her family home. She often dreamed about what it would be like to set up housekeeping in a caboose or freight car—the situation the Alden children find themselves in.

While the mystery element is central to each of Miss Warner's books, she never thought of them as strictly juvenile mysteries. She liked to stress the Aldens' independence and resourcefulness and their solid New England devotion to using up and making do. The Aldens go about most of their adventures with as little adult supervision as possible—something else that delights young readers.

Miss Warner lived in Putnam, Connecticut, until her death in 1979. During her lifetime, she received hundreds of letters from girls and boys telling her how much they liked her books.